# IZZY the INVENTOR

## and the Unexpected Unicorn

# USBORNE QUICKLINKS

DISCOVER EXPERIMENTS LIKE THE ONES IZZY TRIES IN THIS BOOK AND FIND OUT MORE ABOUT THE SCIENCE BEHIND THEM...

AT USBORNE QUICKLINKS WE HAVE PROVIDED LINKS TO WEBSITES WHERE YOU CAN:

• Watch video clips of slime-making experiments.

• See amazing crystals made from simple ingredients.

• Watch how to build a toy raft using twigs, leaves and other natural materials.

• Find lots more experiments to try at home.

TO VISIT THESE SITES, GO TO USBORNE.COM/QUICKLINKS AND TYPE IN THE KEYWORDS "IZZY AND THE UNICORN" OR SCAN THE QR CODE ON THIS PAGE.

PLEASE FOLLOW THE INTERNET SAFETY GUIDELINES AT USBORNE QUICKLINKS.

CHILDREN SHOULD BE SUPERVISED ONLINE.

USBORNE

# Izzy the Inventor
## and the Unexpected Unicorn

Zanna Davidson

ILLUSTRATED BY ELISSA ELWICK

# Contents

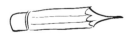

# CHAPTER ONE
# IZZY does <u>not</u> believe in magic

Izzy **loved** science and had big dreams. She wanted to be the GREATEST INVENTOR of all time!

Every day, Izzy put on her lab glasses and her lab coat and set to work on her incredible experiments...

Izzy had notebooks **full** of inventions and experiments.

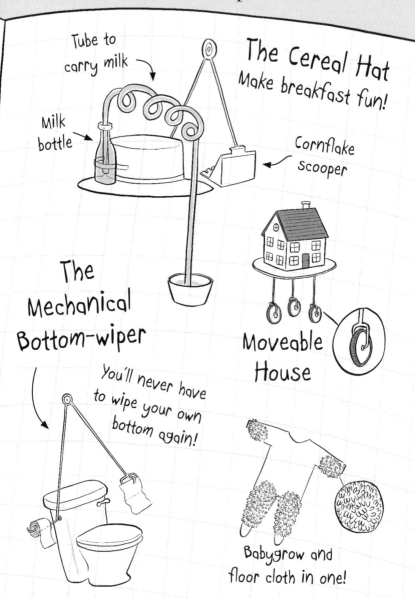

Tube to carry milk

The Cereal Hat
Make breakfast fun!

Milk bottle

Cornflake scooper

The Mechanical Bottom-wiper

Moveable House

You'll never have to wipe your own bottom again!

Babygrow and floor cloth in one!

## The Ear Enhancer

- listen in on secret conversations

## The Dogbrella

- for dogs who hate rain

## Recipe for fake snot
### - just for fun!

Hot water * a bowl * gelatin powder
* green food dye * golden syrup
* a tablespoon and a fork

Put 1 tablespoon of hot water into a bowl with 3 tablespoons of gelatin powder and mix together. Then add a few drops of food dye.

Add 1/2 tablespoon of golden syrup and keep stirring until the mixture becomes stringy and snot-like! Have fun pulling up your strands of fake snot with the fork.

But after the incident of the
**flying egg**...

...the **cereal shower**...

...and the **self-watering plant pot**...

...Izzy's parents decided they'd had enough.

"No more experiments in the house," said Izzy's dad.

"Just for once," said her mum, "I'd like to go to work without fried egg on my face."

"This has got to stop," Izzy's mum went on. "Things are getting out of hand."

Last week there was slime splattered on the ceiling.

A rocket through the window...

"And bouncing eggs down the stairs," said Izzy's little sister, Bella.

"Today, I want you to play with your sister instead," said Izzy's dad.

"Hooray!" cried Bella. "Let's have a fairy tea party!"

You can be the pink fairy, Izzy.

"But I don't *want* to play fairies," cried Izzy. "This isn't fair!"

And she **stomped** up to her room and shut the door.

"I hate being the odd one out in my family. No one else is even **INTERESTED** in science. They don't care about my experiments." Suddenly, Izzy heard a tinkly voice.

It is I, Rose Petal Twinkle-Toes, your Fairy Godmother.

"This can't be happening," said Izzy. "Fairies aren't real. Every scientist knows that."

"You have so much to learn," said the fairy.

Life isn't just about science. Imagination is very important, too.

"Who says so?" asked Izzy.

"A very famous scientist," the fairy replied, and she began writing sparkly words in the air.

Imagination is even more important than knowledge.

Albert Einstein

"What you need," said
the fairy, in a serious voice,
"is a unicorn."

Izzy shook her head. "I'd
much rather you gave me
a science lab."

But the
fairy **WASN'T**
listening.

She was
muttering a spell
beneath her breath.

The air in Izzy's room began to

*sparkle* and *shimmer*.

The next moment, there was a faint **POP!** and a large, plump unicorn appeared in Izzy's bedroom.

"I don't even *believe* in unicorns," said Izzy.

"Oh, the unicorn's real," said the fairy. "Now, follow me!"

On those words, the fairy floated out of the window...

...and headed straight for a cloud of pink mist that was shimmering at the end of the garden.

Izzy took a deep breath. "A proper scientist investigates everything," she declared.

She picked up her notebook and her science bag. Then she looked at Henry for a moment, just to make sure he *really was real*, and jumped onto his back.

He felt very warm and very soft. "Here goes," thought Izzy, and she pointed at the open window, crying...

Follow that fairy!

## CHAPTER TWO
# Fairytale Land

The unicorn was VERY good at following instructions.

On Izzy's command...

...he **leaped** out of the window...

...**bounded** through the garden...

...and **sailed** through
the shimmery
pink mist.

Rapunzel
in her tower...

Jack climbing his
beanstalk...

...and Cinderella
waiting for her prince.

"Fairytale Land is full of fairy creatures too," Henry went on. "There are pixies, imps, elves and... Oh, look! Here come the Rhyming Rabbits."

We're the Rhyming Rabbits!

We're rhyming out of habit.

We rhyme all day, it is our way,

Hooray for rhyming rabbits!

"There must be a scientific explanation for this," thought Izzy. "Maybe I've travelled to another universe!"

Izzy immediately began rifling through her science notebook.

# ARE THERE OTHER UNIVERSES OUT THERE AND CAN I GET TO THEM?

## A scientific paper by IZZY

1. Our universe may be one of many, like a slice of bread in a huge cosmic loaf.

This idea is called the 'Many Worlds Theory'.

Lots of universes, like slices of bread in a giant cosmic loaf.

2. We might be able to reach these other universes if we can find a way in.

**3.** A famous scientist called Stephen Hawking said we might be able to travel to other universes through...

# ...BLACK HOLES.

*A black hole*

Have I fallen into a black hole?

"Um, I think there's been a mistake," said Izzy. "I'm not **Unicorn Girl**. This fairy, called Rose Petal *Something*-Toes came, and..."

At that moment, Rose Petal Twinkle-Toes fluttered over to Izzy.

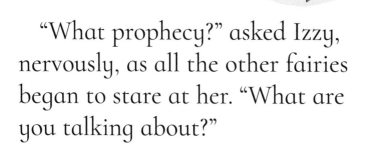

Here is the girl, just as the prophecy said.

"What prophecy?" asked Izzy, nervously, as all the other fairies began to stare at her. "What are you talking about?"

Behind Fairy Rose Petal came
a cloud of yet more fairies,
all carrying a large book.

It's all written
down in the
Magic Tome.

One day a girl will
come on a unicorn.

Her name is Unicorn Girl
and she will save the world
of fairy tales.

But it was **YOU** who gave *me* the unicorn.

"Never mind that now," said Fairy Rose Petal. "Prince Charming is in trouble and it's **YOUR** job to rescue him."

"But I don't know anything about fairy tales," said Izzy.

You've picked the wrong girl!

"How am I meant to save the world of fairy tales?" asked Izzy. "You have your **BRAINS** and a **UNICORN**," replied Fairy Rose Petal. "You can't fail."

Prince Charming is trapped on the Mountain of Doom.

Mountain of Doom this way ←

"Your mission is to bring Prince Charming back to the Royal Palace **TONIGHT**," said Fairy Rose Petal, "in time for the Royal Ball..."

"If he doesn't appear *before* sunset," she went on, "Cinderella will have no one to dance with and fairy tales everywhere will be RUINED."

"That's fine by me," said Izzy. "I'd much rather read a science book than a *fairy tale* any day."

The fairies started to laugh. All at the same time. It was like a hundred **HIGH-PITCHED** silver bells going off at once.

Ha ha haaaa

Ha ha Haaaa

Ha ha haaaa

Ha ha Haaaa

Ha ha haaaa

Ha ha haaaa

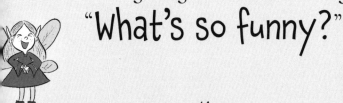

"What's going on?" asked Izzy.
"What's so funny?"

"I don't think you understand, dear," said Fairy Rose Petal, who had **STOPPED** laughing as suddenly as she'd begun. Her voice didn't sound at all tinkly now.

You can't leave Fairytale Land until you've found the prince.

Izzy **gulped.**

"A quest!" cried Henry. "Hooray!"

I do love a quest!

# CHAPTER THREE
# SLIME TROLLS

Izzy sat on the ground in despair. "This *cannot* be happening," she sighed.

I'm stuck here until I rescue Prince Charming, aren't I?

Yup.

"But really," said Henry, doing a little tap dance of excitement, "if you think about it, we're so lucky! Rescuing a prince is such an important mission. Let's check the map."

Izzy opened it up to look.

"Gosh," she said, after a moment. "The Mountain of Doom is further away than it looks..."

45

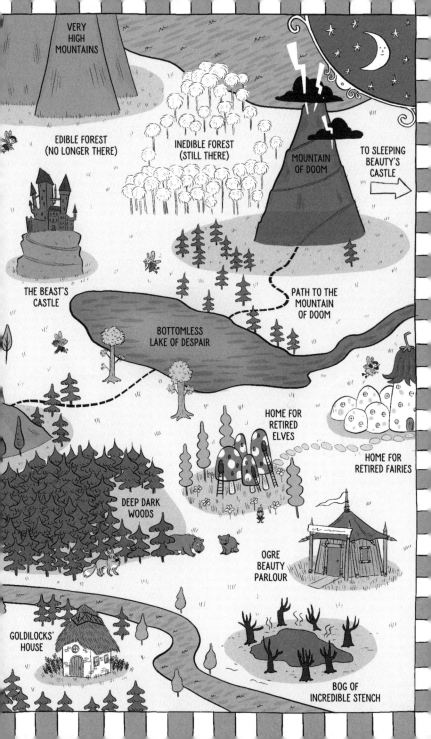

Izzy realized, however, that she had NO CHOICE.

"Okay," said Izzy, "let's do this. After all, how hard can it be to rescue a prince?"

"Hooray!" said Henry. "This is my best day EVER! Onto my back, Izzy."

First stop, the Bridge of Angry Trolls.

But as they set off, the Rhyming Rabbits started to sing again.

"The wicked troll called Mary?"
Izzy asked the Rhyming Rabbits.
"Who's she?"
"She's the **TROLL QUEEN!**"
chorused the rabbits.

She's green!
And mean!

And mighty!
And bitey!

"Oh no," said Henry.
"You've set them off again."

She's forty.

And warty!

Izzy wanted to ask more questions, but Henry had already begun trotting over the bridge.

I'm feeling a bit nervous about these trolls.

Don't worry! We're in Fairytale Land.

What could possibly go wrong?

An extremely large troll had stepped onto the bridge. It shuddered beneath her weight.

The troll was green and fierce-looking, with a spiky crown and big, yellow teeth. Izzy guessed she was probably called Mary.

What do you want?

Um, we'd like to cross your bridge, if that's okay?

"Firstly," said the troll, "you must address me as **Troll Queen Mary**. And secondly, the answer is **NO**, it's not okay. You can't cross our bridge – not unless you **FIGHT US**."

At the word 'fight' the trolls started jumping up and down and shaking their enormous fists.

Henry twirled on one leg. A beautiful, shimmering rainbow swooshed out from his horn. But the trolls didn't seem to notice...

Fight Fight!

"There must be something we can do," thought Izzy. Then she caught sight of the sign.

"Troll Queen Mary," said Izzy, trying to make herself heard over the chanting. "Why are you so **ANGRY**?"

"Because we have lost our slime!" said Mary.

Once we had all the slime we wanted.

"Those were **happy times**," said Mary...

We played in slime!

We bathed in slime!

We fought with slime.

"But then," sobbed Mary, "the fairies took our slime away!"

"I can make slime for you!" said Izzy, taking her notebook from her bag. "I know just the right experiment!"

# SLIME!

All you need to make **SLIME** is some PVA glue, baking soda and contact lens solution. You can add food dye and vinegar, too, if you want.

Glue on its own is sticky but drippy. To make slime, you need to make the glue actually stick to itself in a big ball that you can pull apart and squeeze together. That's what the baking soda and contact lens solution are for. They make the glue more GLOOPY!

## My notes about slime:

**SLIME** is amazing as it isn't a solid or a liquid — it's somewhere in between. You can pick it up like a solid but it also OOZES like a liquid. And it changes shape to fill whatever container you put it in. You can also bounce it like a ball!

If you pull slime slowly, it stretches. But if you pull it quickly it will break apart more easily.

**IMPORTANT:**
SLIME IS **NOT** FOR EATING!!

I think I've got all the ingredients. I just need a really large pot.

Troll Queen Mary reached into her pocket and pulled out a large, leather-bound tome. Then she began to read...

One day a girl will come and give you back the joy of slime.

Her name is Slime Girl.

Izzy wasn't sure she liked
the sound of **Slime Girl**, but
she wasn't going to say so.
"If I make this slime for you, do
you promise to let us pass?"

"We promise," said Mary, and
handed Izzy an enormous pot.

The trolls were very **EXCITED**.

Izzy set to work. She stirred and mixed and squished until she had a **HUGE LUMP** of stretchy green **slime**. Izzy checked her recipe. "Just one more ingredient..."

Now for the vinegar!

All of a sudden, the slime began **swelling** and **fizzing** and **bubbling** and then with a **big BANG** it...

"Izzy!" whispered Henry. "The trolls seem very happy. I think now is the time to leave!"

Before the trolls could change their minds, Izzy and Henry trotted across the bridge, and continued on their quest...

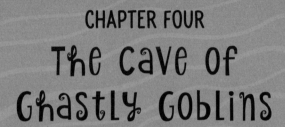

# CHAPTER FOUR
# The Cave of Ghastly Goblins

"There's no such thing as magic," insisted Izzy. "That was **science**."

She wanted to explain it all to Henry, but by now they had reached the entrance to a dark tunnel. There was a sign outside, painted black.

We just need to pop through here and out the other side.

CAVE OF **GHASTLY GOBLINS** THIS WAY ←

"**GHASTLY GOBLINS**?" said Izzy, reading the sign.

"What fun!" said Henry.

Izzy and Henry followed
the path as it wound **deeper**
and **deeper**...

It got **darker**
and **darker**...

"I'll just get out my torch," said Izzy.

Then she almost wished she hadn't...

"Sorry," said Izzy. "We're on our way to the Mountain of Doom."

The Ghastly Goblins let out a long, low cackle that bounced off the cave walls. "You **CANNOT** pass through," they said, "unless you give us **something in return**."

Izzy thought fast. "I can make crystals. I know the science experiment. Would that do?"

"One for each of us?" asked the greedy goblins.

"It's a deal," said Izzy. "But first, I need some hot water."

The goblins passed her a cup of water from a bubbling cauldron. Izzy set to work...

"Now we put it somewhere cold," said Izzy, going to the coldest, darkest corner of the cave.

"About three hours," said Izzy. "But it'll be worth it."

"This science thing is **SO slow**," complained the goblins.

"I know!" said Henry. "I'll sing to pass the time."

At last, the **CRYSTALS** were ready...

"I am **NOT** a horned horse," humphed Henry.

"And I'm really *not* magic," insisted Izzy. "You see, the Epsom salts dissolve in the water. As the water cools, the atoms in the salt start joining together to make crystals..."

But the goblins weren't listening.

Mine's the best!

No, mine is!

They were too busy gazing at their glittering crystals.

"We must hurry," said Izzy. "We're running out of time."

Remember — we've got to get Prince Charming back before sunset.

You're right. Where to next?

Izzy and Henry checked the map. "Oh no," said Izzy. "I'm not sure I like the sound of our next stop." She read in big black letters...

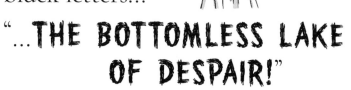

"...THE BOTTOMLESS LAKE OF DESPAIR!"

# CHAPTER FIVE
# THE BOTTOMLESS LAKE OF DESPAIR

When they arrived at the lake, Izzy and Henry felt slightly daunted.

It's a shame I'm not a very strong swimmer...

The lake was **very long** and **very wide**.

THE
BOTTOMLESS
LAKE OF
DESPAIR

"We'll just have to fly across," said Izzy.

"I can't fly," said Henry, sadly. "I can only sort of... **flutter**."

"In that case," said Izzy, smiling at him, "I'll build us a raft. Watch and see!"

"Shall I add some glitter?"
asked Henry.
"Definitely!" said Izzy.

"*Ta da!*" said Izzy, when at last
the raft was done. "Now we can
cross the lake."

"Are you sure this will work?"
asked Henry.

Not exactly...

"I've only made a toy raft
before," admitted Izzy. "And that
was in the bath."

They both stepped gingerly onto
the raft.

"It's working!"
cried Henry, jumping
up and down in
excitement.

"Stop!" cried Izzy,
as the raft began
WIBBLING...

...and **WOBBLING!**

It rocked from side to side.

"Oh no!" said Henry. "What have I done? *Whoah!* I'm losing my balance..."

"Me too!" said Izzy. And with

a SPLASH they fell into the water.

Izzy began laughing. "Look!" she said, standing up. "It turns out the Bottomless Lake of Despair isn't bottom-less after all. It isn't even **deep**. We can just **WALK** across it!"

Mountain of Doom, here we come!

But when they
reached the other side,
the sun was very low in
the sky.

"Uh oh!" said Henry.
"Not long till
sunset..."

We're never
going to make
it to the top of
the mountain
in time.

"It's all my fault. This never would have happened if I were a **proper** unicorn," said Henry.

The trolls didn't like my Rainbow of Peace.

The goblins loathed my singing.

And then *I* CAPSIZED the raft.

"I've failed you, Izzy," sobbed Henry. "I'm a USELESS unicorn."

"You haven't failed me," said Izzy. "I think you're a wonderful unicorn."

All I'm good for is glitter and dancing.

"I'M NOT WONDERFUL," said Henry, tearfully. "All the other unicorns in Fairytale Land  can do amazing magic."

In despair, Henry **plunged** his horn into the **mountainside**.

All at once, there was a loud
**PING!** and a secret door in the
mountain slid open.

A voice spoke to them.

Welcome to the
Mountain of
Doom. Please
enter the lift
if you would
like a ride.

"Hooray!" cried Izzy, flinging her
arms around Henry. "You've saved
us! There's a **LIFT**!"

They stepped inside and the
doors closed behind them. The lift
shot up at full speed.

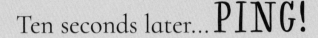

Ten seconds later... **PING!**

> You have reached your destination. We do hope you enjoyed your journey.

A nervous-looking man stepped forward to greet them. "Prince Charming?" said Izzy.

> Yes, it is I.

We've come to rescue you and take you to the Royal Palace.

"You must be so **overjoyed** to see us!" said Henry, grinning.

But Prince Charming didn't look very happy to see them. Quite the opposite, in fact.

He beckoned them into a little hallway, where he began wringing his hands.

"*Oh dear, oh dear,*" he muttered. "I really hoped no one would find me here."

"You see, I know what happens if I go to the ball..." sighed Prince Charming. "First, I have to dance with Cinderella, and I *hate* dancing!"

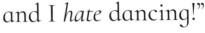

96

"Then I have to run about with a glass slipper trying to *find* Cinderella...

Lastly, I have to marry her! I don't even **KNOW HER!**

I just want to be left alone to become a lepidopterist."

A lep-i-WHAT-terist?

It's someone who studies moths and butterflies.

"So I'm afraid you've wasted your time," said the prince decisively, and began ushering them back into the lift.

"I'm **NOT** going to the Royal Ball and you **CAN'T MAKE ME!**"

"But if you don't go to the Royal Ball," said Izzy, her voice starting to wobble, "then I'll **NEVER** get home."

# CHAPTER SIX
## Happily Ever After

Izzy didn't know what to do. She had to make the prince change his mind.

I don't know any science that can help me.

Izzy looked pleadingly at Henry.
He was her only hope.

The thing is,
you might not
*want* to go to
the Royal Ball...

"But what about *Cinderella*?"
Henry said to Prince Charming.
"Don't you think it would be polite
to explain it to her?"

Oh golly, I
suppose you're right...
and I was brought up
to have good manners.
Fine. I'll come with you.
But *NO* dancing.

"We don't have much time," said Izzy, "if we're going to get there before sunset. Let's go!"

Izzy and the prince leaped onto Henry's back, and away they went.

Down the lift to the bottom of the **Mountain of Doom**...

Across the (not so) **Bottomless Lake of Despair**...

Through the
**Cave of Ghastly Goblins**...

Over the
**Bridge of** (much less)
**Angry Trolls**...

And up the steps of the Royal Palace, just as the sun was about to set...

The prince rushed through a cloud of fairies, and called out to the girl on the palace steps.

"Yoo hoo!" he called. "Helloooo! Cin-der-rell-aaaaa!"

The girl on the steps turned and looked back in surprise.

"Prince Charming?" she said. "We're not meant to have met yet!"

Cinderella! I have to talk to you.

I'm sorry but I can't go to the ball. I hate dancing.

The prince raced up the last of the steps until he was standing by Cinderella's side.

"I think it would be fun to run a kingdom," said Cinderella, smiling up at the prince.

At home, I already do the cooking, the cleaning...

...the laundry and the accounts...

Running a kingdom would be a doddle.

"In that case, would you like to go to the Royal Ball with me and **NOT** dance?" asked the prince.

"I would be delighted," said Cinderella, beaming.

Wait! This isn't how the fairy tale ends!

"I think it's a brilliant ending. Everyone's happy," said Izzy.

"But there at least has to be dancing," said the fairy.

That's not a problem. Follow me!

Henry
**GALLOPED**
into the ballroom
and gave the finest
dance of his life.

After the ball was over, Izzy felt a tap on her shoulder. "You can go home now," said Fairy Rose Petal. "I thought 𝓕airytale 𝓛and needed some of your brilliant science, and I was right! But I want you to **promise** me something..."

"What is it?" asked Izzy. She knew you couldn't be too careful with fairies...

I want you to come back if we need your help.

Umm...

"Everyone needs a little magic in their life sometimes," said Fairy Rose Petal.

"Then I promise," said Izzy. "I'll come whenever you need me."

Izzy turned to give Henry a hug.

Then Fairy Rose Petal waved her wand and in a **flash...**

...Izzy was back in her bedroom...

...just as her sister **burst** through the door.

"Really?" said Bella.

"Everyone needs a little magic in their life sometimes..." said Izzy.

Izzy and Bella played together for the rest of the day. Izzy even put on a pair of Bella's fairy wings, and spoke in a tinkly voice – just as she'd heard the fairies speak.

That night, as Izzy lay in bed, she spotted a copy of Cinderella in the corner of her room. She went over to pick it up.

I'll just check the last page.

"I haven't read the story for a long time," thought Izzy, "but the ending has definitely... **CHANGED**."

She smiled to herself. She was pretty sure the new ending was *even better* than the old one.

# Cinderella

"I don't want to go to the Royal Ball," said the prince. "I hate dancing."

"Oh, me too!" cried Cinderella.

"Well in that case," said the prince, "would you like to go to the Royal Ball with me and NOT dance?"

"Yes please," said Cinderella.

# Cinderella

In time, Cinderella and the prince
fell in love and were married.

The prince became a famous
lepidopterist while Cinderella ruled
the kingdom wisely and well.

And, once a year,
they had a Royal Ball,
in celebration of
Henry, the amazing
dancing unicorn.

What a great
ending!

# Cinderella

But did they all live Happily Ever After? No! They did not! Cinderella and Prince Charming had forgotten to invite BAD FAIRY BRENDA to their wedding.

She was so **ANGRY** she put a curse on all the other fairy tales.

"I'll start with Sleeping Beauty," snarled Brenda. "Even true love's kiss can't wake her now."

"Then what can?" asked a good fairy.

# Cinderella

"Nothing!" snapped Brenda.

"Come on," said the good fairy.

"Okay," sighed Brenda. "Sleeping Beauty can wake... but only when it snows in the Forever Summer Meadows AND," she added, pointing at Henry, "that unicorn can fly."

The good fairies were in great distress.

"Help!" they said. "We need Unicorn Girl! Only she can save us..."

GULP!

## The End

Here are some experiments from Izzy's *science notebook...*

# Make Bouncing Eggs

(This experiment is best done on a hard fl[...]

1. Take a whole egg (uncooked).

2. Leave it in a jug of white vinegar for 2-3 days.

3. Wash or scrub away any shell that is left.

4. Hold the egg 2.5 - 5cm above the ground.

5. Let go, and watch it bounce.

6. See how high you can drop the egg before it splats!

## How it works:

The shell of a chicken egg is made of a hard material called calcium carbonate. Vinegar is a type of acid, which reacts with calcium carbonate. Over time, the vinegar dissolves the egg shell, and then gets to work on the thin skin covering the egg under the shell. The vinegar makes the skin tougher, which in turn makes the egg bouncy.

# Make EXPLODING slime   by Izzy

## What you'll need:

- 118ml bottle of PVA washable school glue
- Baking Soda (also known as bicarbonate of soda)
- Food dye (optional)
- White vinegar
- Contact lens solution

## How to make slime:

Squeeze the glue into a bowl. Sprinkle over 1/4 teaspoon of baking soda and mix it in with a spoon. Add a few drops of food dye if you want colour, then add a few drops of the contact lens solution. Mix it together with the spoon. Keep adding a few drops of the contact lens solution at a time, and keep mixing it in, until you have a stringy ball. Then start kneading the slime with your hands until it's less sticky but still stretchy.

## Now make it explode!

Push down the middle of your slime to create a hole and add 1/2 tablespoon of baking soda. Mix it in with your hands. Repeat about 5 or 6 times until the slime starts to stiffen and feel a bit gritty.

The more baking soda you add, the better the reaction!

Put the slime in a bowl and make it into a volcano shape.

Pour in a bit of vinegar and then a little more...

step back and watch it explode!

# Grow Your Own Needle Crystals
## by Izzy

## What you need:

A cup or small bowl

1/2 cup of hot tap water

 1/2 cup Epsom salts (magnesium sulfate)

A drop of food dye (Optional)

## Interesting facts:

Epsom salt isn't actually a salt at all! It's a mineral called magnesium sulfate. When you add it to warm water, magnesium sulfate starts to dissolve and combine with the water. But as the water cools down, it separates from the water again, and starts clumping together to make crystals.

## What to do:

1. Pour warm water into a cup or bowl.

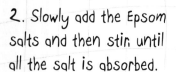

2. Slowly add the Epsom salts and then stir until all the salt is absorbed.

There might be a bit of salt left at the bottom, but that's okay.

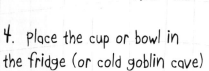

3. Add a drop of food dye.

4. Place the cup or bowl in the fridge (or cold goblin cave) and leave it for 3 hours.

If you want to speed things up, you can put the solution in your freezer first, for about 10 minutes.

5. The crystals will now slowly start to form.

The longer you leave them in the fridge, the bigger they'll be.

Once they are a few centimetres long, you can carefully scoop them out and keep them in a jar.

They'll last longer if you keep them in a jar with a lid or top.

# Build A Toy Raft

## A step-by-step guide
## by Izzy

### What you need:

- 2 thick sticks for the base

- About 10 smaller sticks for the raft deck
  (all sticks should be about the same length)

- Twine or string to tie it together

- Scissors

### What to do:

1. Put down the thick sticks, lying
   horizontally a little distance
   apart, and then put one of the
   raft deck sticks on top of them,
   on the left hand side.

2. Cut a long section of twine
   (at least a metre) and tie
   the first stick to the base.

**3.** Wind the twine around the sticks twice one way, and then do the same the other way, forming a cross to hold the sticks in place.

**4.** Continue doing this, joining up the sticks along one side of the raft. Pull tight between each twig.

**5.** Do the same to the ends of the twigs on the other side of the raft, put it on water and see how it floats!

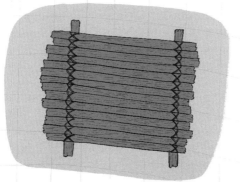

## SCIENCE SAFETY

ALWAYS TAKE EXTRA CARE WITH HOT OR SHARP THINGS
AND NEVER PUT ANYTHING IN YOUR MOUTH. IF AN
ACTIVITY INVOLVES DOING SOMETHING YOU MIGHT NOT
USUALLY DO, ASK YOUR GROWN-UP TO HELP YOU.

Series designer: Brenda Cole

Series editor: Lesley Sims

Cover design by Freya Harrison
and Hannah Cobley

Digital manipulation by Nick Wakeford